MOVE IT,
Miss Macintosh!

By Peggy Robbins Janousky

Art by Meghan Lands

annick press
toronto + berkeley + vancouver

Miss Macintosh woke up one morning certain of two things:

1) It was the first day of school.
2) She wasn't going.

"I think I'll just stay home today,"
said Miss Macintosh as she snuggled
back under the covers.

The sound of the doorbell
jolted her out of bed.

Ding Dong!

Rise and Shine, Miss Macintosh!

said Principal Bellwether
in a booming voice.

"Principal Bellwether?
What are you doing here?"

"I should be asking
you the same
  question,"
he said.

Miss Macintosh crawled back to bed and pulled the blankets up over her head.

"Just as I suspected," said Principal Bellwether. "You've got a bad case of the butterflies. All kindergarten teachers get them. Last year I had a terrible time when Mr. Jitters started school. He cried so much I had to call his mother."

"I've taken the liberty of picking out your clothes," called Mrs. Sketcher, the art teacher. "I admire your creativity, but Pajama Day isn't till spring."

Miss Macintosh looked at the outfit and gasped.

Where was her purple bow? Where was her sparkly new dress??

Where was her lucky apple necklace???

"I think I'll get dressed by myself," said Miss Macintosh. And she did.

Time for breakfast!

bellowed Mrs. Burger, the lunch lady.

"I'm not hungry!" said Miss Macintosh.

"Nonsense," said Mrs. Burger.
"How do you expect to teach your
children on an empty stomach?"

"I don't," she mumbled.

Miss Macintosh
pushed her cereal
around with
her spoon.

She squished it,
and squashed it,
and squished
it again.

"Playing with your food won't get you out of going to school," said Mr. Jitters. "I tried the same thing last year. I missed the bus and my father had to drive me. Principal Bellwether had a fit."

Miss Macintosh grabbed her cereal and slurped it down in no time flat.

"Ready," she said.

"The only thing you're
ready for is a cavity," said
Mr. Comfort, the school nurse.

Miss Macintosh raced for
her toothbrush.

"Don't forget to floss,"
he called through the door.

Miss Macintosh looked in the mirror and sighed.

Her dress was new and sparkly.

Her teeth were clean and shiny.

Her stomach was full
of good food.

She felt awful.

School is not for me, thought Miss Macintosh as she slipped out the bathroom door.

"Where do you think you're going?" asked Ms. Patience, the guidance counselor.

"Back to bed," said Miss Macintosh. "I don't feel like being new today."

"Everyone's new in kindergarten," said
Ms. Patience. "Everyone's in the same boat."

"I know a song about a boat!" announced
Miss Melody, the music teacher. "I always
sing it when I'm nervous. Would you
like to hear it?"

Miss Melody began
to sing at the top
of her lungs:

We're in the Same boat, We're both kind of New.

So let's stick together just like paper and glue!

"What a lovely song," said Miss Macintosh.

"Wait till you hear the rest of it," chirped Miss Melody.

"No time," yelled Principal Bellwether. "The bus is here!"

Move it, Miss Macintosh!

Miss Macintosh grabbed her lunch box and charged out the door. She didn't slow down till she reached the bus.

"I thought you might be late this morning,"
said Miss Bluebird, the school bus driver.
"Find a seat and keep your feet out of the aisle.
By the way, dear, your shoelace is untied."

"I don't know how to tie my shoes,"
whispered Miss Macintosh.

"No worries," tweeted Miss Bluebird.
"Kindergarten is the perfect place to learn."

Miss Macintosh's thoughts turned like the wheels on the bus.

What if she couldn't find her classroom?

What if she couldn't open her lunch??

What if no one liked her???

When the bus came to a
stop, so did Miss Macintosh.

"School is not for me," she groaned.

Miss Macintosh tiptoed down the hall and peeked into the classroom.

Twenty-two pairs of terrified eyes peeked back.

"Good morning, children," she said as she inched her way into the room. "My name is Miss Macintosh."

Oh no, thought Miss Macintosh. Why isn't anyone answering? Could the children have butterflies too?

She tried to remember the words
to Miss Melody's song, but she
was just too nervous.

Instead, she sang the first thing
that popped into her head.

"I tried to stay home.

I hid in my bed.

I love apple jelly.

Wish my hair was bright red."

From the back of the class, Miss Macintosh heard
a small giggle. Her heart soared with hope.

Keep singing! she told herself.

"I can't tie my shoes.

The cat ate my socks.

Can we go home early?

Oh my gosh, they have blocks!"

The giggle spread from row to row until the
whole room was buzzing with laughter.

When Miss Macintosh looked up,
she was certain of two things:

1) It was the first day of school.
2) She was going to love it after all.

Edited by Debbie Rogosin
Designed by Belle Wuthrich

Annick Press Ltd.

We acknowledge the support of the Canada Council for the Arts,
the Ontario Arts Council, and the participation of the Government of Canada/
la participation du gouvernement du Canada for our publishing activities.

ONTARIO ARTS COUNCIL
CONSEIL DES ARTS DE L'ONTARIO
an Ontario government agency
un organisme du gouvernement de l'Ontario

Funded by the
Government
of Canada

Financé par le
gouvernement
du Canada

Canadä

To my family, who always
believed that I would make it to
kindergarten. With much love
—P.J.

Big thank-yous to Ashley Spires
—M.L.

Cataloging in Publication
Robbins Janousky, Peggy, author
      Move it, Miss Macintosh! / Peggy Robbins Janousky ; art by
Meghan Lands.

Issued in print and electronic formats.
ISBN 978-1-55451-863-0 (hardcover).—ISBN 978-1-55451-862-3 (paperback).
—ISBN 978-1-55451-864-7 (html).—ISBN 978-1-55451-865-4 (pdf)

      I. Lands, Meghan, 1984–, illustrator II. Title.

PZ7.1 J35 Mo 2016   j813'.6   C2016-900595-X
                                                C2016-900596-8

Distributed in Canada by University of Toronto Press.
Published in the U.S.A. by Annick Press (U.S.) Ltd.
Distributed in the U.S.A. by Publishers Group West.

Printed in China

Visit us at: www.annickpress.com
Visit Peggy Robbins Janousky at: PeggyInPrint.com
Visit Meghan Lands at: meghanlands.com

Also available in e-book format.
Please visit www.annickpress.com/ebooks.html for more details. Or scan